PUPPY PATROL

ABANDONED!

PUPPY PATROL

ABANDONED!

JENNY DALE

Illustrations by Mick Reid
Cover illustration by Michael Rowe

AN
APPLE
PAPERBACK

SCHOLASTIC INC.
New York Toronto London Auckland Sydney
Mexico City New Delhi Hong Kong

SPECIAL THANKS TO LINDA KEMPTON

No part of this publication may be reproduced in whole or in part, or stored in a retrieval system, or transmitted in any form or by any means, electronic, mechanical, photocopying, recording, or otherwise, without written permission of the publisher. For information regarding permission, write to Macmillan Publishers Ltd., 25 Eccleston Place, London SW1W 9NF, and Basingstoke.

ISBN 0-439-11325-3

All rights reserved. Published by Scholastic Inc., 555 Broadway, New York, NY 10012, by arrangement with Macmillan Children's Books, a division of Macmillan Publishers Ltd.

SCHOLASTIC and associated logos are trademarks and/or registered trademarks of Scholastic Inc.

12 11 10 9 8 7 6 5 4 3   0 1 2 3 4 5/0

Printed in the U.S.A.   40
First Scholastic printing, January 2000

It was eight-thirty in the evening when a loud knock on the Parkers' front door startled everyone.

Sam barked noisily and ran into the hallway. Five-year-old Sarah stomped after him, giggling excitedly.

"I'll get it!" Neil laughed. "Quiet, Sam! And that goes for you, too, Squirt!"

He tore himself away from the police drama he had been watching on TV and followed his excitable Border collie and equally high-spirited little sister to the door.

A tall stranger stood in the glow of their security light. The dark shadows cast on his face by the powerful beam made it difficult for Neil to see him properly. But it was light enough to see the large, hairy brown dog sitting obediently at the man's side.

"Can I help you?" asked Neil. He shivered a little as a blast of cold air blew in from outside.

"Well, I hope so," said the stranger. "Is this King Street Kennels?"

"Yes," replied Neil.

"I need to see someone about boarding my dog . . ."

"I'm afraid the kennels are closed now. We open again at eight tomorrow morning." Neil couldn't keep the edge of annoyance out of his voice. He hated it when people came at strange hours to leave their dogs. They seemed to have no idea about the way professional kennels were run.

"This is really an emergency. Perhaps I could talk to your father?"

At that moment Bob Parker came up behind Neil.

"What's the problem?" he asked quietly.

Neil backed away from the door, but stayed nearby, his curiosity aroused, and absentmindedly rubbed Sam's ears. They both had a good view of the man's dog, which hadn't moved. It was some kind of crossbreed, thought Neil. Definitely a touch of Airedale. Strangely, it showed no interest in Sam at all, and both man and dog seemed oblivious to the cold, damp October evening.

Neil shifted his gaze to the man again. He wore an expensive-looking gray raincoat and his shiny black hair was perfectly shaped, as if he had just come from the barber. He reminded Neil of the clean-cut hero of one of the old-fashioned black-and-white movies they sometimes showed on day-time TV.

"I had no idea they were going to spring this business trip on me," the man was saying. "Normally, my sister looks after her, but she's visiting friends in Manchester and I have to be at the airport at five-thirty in the morning. Anyway, even though the puppies aren't due for another three weeks, my sister would have been nervous. A friend recommended King Street Kennels."

The man gave them a hopeful look. "I'm prepared to pay double your fee if it will help you make up your mind. . . ."

"That won't be necessary," Mr. Parker replied briskly. "It is rather late, Mr. Harding, but I can see that you're in a genuine fix. In view of the circumstances, of course we'll take Jessie. I'll need a current vaccination certificate for her and a week's boarding fee in advance, if that's OK."

Jessie. So that was the dog's name. While Mr. Harding completed the formalities with his dad, Neil edged out of the doorway and squatted down. He held out his hand cautiously for her to sniff, and when Jessie's tail thumped on the ground to indicate her acceptance of him, he gently rubbed the dog's shaggy chest. She stuck out a long pink tongue to lick his hand.

Mr. Harding looked down at them and smiled. "It looks as if my Jessie has made a new friend already," he observed, ruffling the wiry hair behind Jessie's ears.

"My son has a natural affinity with dogs, Mr. Harding," said Bob Parker. "I can assure you that she will be in excellent hands here. And you don't have to worry about Jessie's condition. We've had pregnant dogs here before and we know what level of nutrition and exercise they need."

A relieved expression crossed Mr. Harding's face. "Fine. Well, thanks again. I'm sure Jessie will be well cared for. I'll try to call from Tokyo to see how she's doing, but it might be a little difficult, what with the time difference and the fact that I'll be tied up in meetings . . ." He bent down to give Jessie a final pat. "Bye, Jess. It's only for a week and then I'll be back. Be a good girl."

He handed her leash to Bob and turned, walking away briskly toward his mud-splashed white van without looking back. The grubbiness of the vehicle seemed at odds with the immaculate appearance of its driver. Neil stared as the brake lights glowed red. His eyes followed the van as it crackled down the gravel drive, then, with a shrug, he turned his attention back to their new guest.

Jessie stood, slowly wagging her huge, feathery tail and whining softly, as if willing her master to change his mind and come back for her.

Neil placed his hand on the dog's head to comfort her.

"Daddy, Daddy, that man was —" Sarah began.

"I've told you a dozen times that it's rude to stare at people, Sarah," said Mrs. Parker, walking up the hallway toward them.

"But he had funny hair, Mommy!"

"Don't be silly, dear. Now, run upstairs. It's way past your bedtime!"

Sarah started her usual bedtime pouts and protests.

"Is it OK if I kennel Jessie?" asked Neil, anxious to escape from Sarah's whines.

"Yes, of course," his mother replied. "I'll come along to the office and write up her card."

King Street Kennels and Rescue Center was located behind the Parkers' house and garden. The fields and meadows that lay beyond were ideal for exercising the dogs. Compton town center was a couple of miles away.

With Sam bounding alongside, Neil took Jessie's leash from his father and made his way across the yard with her to the kennels. Although she had ignored Sam when he had attempted to sniff her on the doorstep, Jessie now wagged her tail and pricked up her ears with interest as the Border collie came near.

"Make friends, Sam," Neil told him.

The two dogs sniffed each other and exchanged doggy greetings. It looked as though they would get along well together.

Sam began to bounce around, trying to interest Jessie in a game. "Sit!" commanded Neil. Sam obeyed immediately but, to Neil's surprise, Jessie sat, too.

Neil decided to conduct an experiment. He knew he was taking a risk and that his parents would be furious if Jessie ran off, but he felt instinctively that she wouldn't. Letting go of her leash, he said, "Stay." Then he walked across the yard.

Sam quivered in his excitement to follow Neil. His whole body was wriggling and his tail was banging the ground. In complete contrast to the Border collie, Jessie sat calmly, not moving at all, her bright brown eyes following Neil, her ears pricked for any order he might be about to give.

"Sam — come, Sam!" Before Neil had finished calling Sam's name for the first time, the dog was off, bounding up to his eleven-year-old master, his pink tongue lolling in a panting grin.

If Neil had expected Jessie to follow in his wake, he was wrong. She was still obeying his command to "stay."

"Jessie. Come now, Jessie." Neil clapped his hands and the brown dog with the shiny black nose trotted up to him.

"Good girl," Neil told her. He gave the new arrival a pat, glanced around to make sure he hadn't been spotted by his mother, and then picked up her leash again. Although it was evening, the yard was quite well lit. But he was in luck — no one had seen him.

They walked over to the kennel block where Jessie was to be housed for the week. Jessie walked perfectly to heel the whole time. Neil was amazed at how well trained she was. She didn't flinch when he opened the outside door to Kennel Block One with a clatter and switched on the lights. Even when a dozen or so dogs all started barking at once, her only reaction was to twitch her ears.

It was the half-term vacation and the kennels were almost full; Jessie was lucky to have secured the last space.

Neil took Jessie into her pen. He released her from her leash and hung it on a hook beside the mesh door. In the fluorescent light, he could see that her hairy coat was mostly a deep golden color, with hints of black along her back, on the tips of her ears, and in her tail feathering. She had an alert, intelligent expression. While Neil went off to get a bowl of fresh water for her, Jessie ran around the pen, sniffing everywhere and investigating her neighbors on each side.

In the office, Neil's mother, Carole, was busy completing the registration card for Jessie. It was important that detailed records were kept of every dog they boarded.

"Should I give Jessie any food tonight?" Neil asked her, sticking his head through the open doorway.

"It's a little late, I think, Neil," she said, "but you might give her a biscuit, just in case she missed a meal. You'll need to get one from the pantry."

The pantry was located between the two kennel blocks and it didn't take Neil long to find what he wanted.

On his way back, he couldn't pass any of the other dogs without having a quick word with each of them.

One special favorite was a gentle German shepherd called King, who was a regular visitor because his owners traveled often.

Most of their boarders settled in quickly. The Parkers gave them plenty of caring attention and exercise, and it was rare that they found a dog too difficult. Bob and Carole usually suggested that new dogs have a one-night stay first, to get them used to the kennels and to prepare them for when their owners went away for a longer period.

Of course, it was a different story for the rescue center. Often these dogs had been so badly treated or neglected that it took the Parkers some time to persuade them to trust human beings again.

Returning to Jessie's pen, Neil found her lying stretched out with her nose between her paws, looking dejected.

"Here you are, Jessie. A special treat for you!" He held out the biscuit to her.

Jessie stood up and came over to examine it. She sniffed and took it gently in her mouth, then dropped it on the floor and turned away.

"Don't you want it?" asked Neil.

She didn't seem the least bit interested, unlike Sam, who was fidgeting at Neil's side, licking his lips and eyeing the biscuit greedily. Jessie flopped down on the floor again, raised her shaggy eyebrows, and gave a big sigh.

Perhaps the puppies were making her tired, Neil

thought. "Don't worry, Jessie. It'll all seem better in the morning," he promised her cheerfully.

Neil switched off the lights and secured the door to the kennel block.

"Come, Sam," he called. "Time for bed!"

Neil awoke to the sound of his sister Sarah singing at the top of her lungs. "Miss Polly had a dolly who was sick, sick, sick," she sang. "So she sent for the doctor to come quick, quick, quick." Then Neil heard her counting the stairs as she went down them. "One step, two steps, three steps, four . . ."

Neil groaned and pushed his head under the pillow. Sarah was always much too lively in the mornings — not Neil's style at all.

Downstairs, Neil's parents were at the big, wooden kitchen table with his other sister, Emily, reading the local newspaper. They were talking about their plans for the day. King Street Kennels was a family business, and the whole family joined in when they could. Bob and Carole also employed a full-time kennel assistant, Kate McGuire.

"We still haven't found homes for Sausage and Mash," said Emily, "so I think it's time the Puppy Patrol stepped in!" The Puppy Patrol was the name Neil's classmates at school had given them, because their whole lives revolved around dogs and the kennels.

"I have a suggestion to make." Emily gazed seriously at her parents to get their attention, but had to wait while Sarah settled herself noisily at her place.

Sausage and Mash were two small mongrel puppies in the rescue center. They were about eight weeks old, and had been left for dead next to an old railroad station. The Parkers hadn't found homes for either of them yet, so Emily had taken them on as her special project.

"Fine," murmured Mr. Parker, buttering more toast. "Let's hear it, then."

"I think we should keep them!" Sarah chipped in, tipping too many cornflakes into her bowl so that some fell on the floor.

Fortunately, Sam was under the table ready to clean up any crumbs.

"Careful, Sarah," said her mother, putting the cereal box safely to one side. "You know we can't have any more pets. Sam and Fudge are quite enough for us."

Emily coughed loudly, annoyed at the interruption. "As I was saying," she continued, "my idea is that we should call Mr. Brooke and ask him to write about them in the *Compton News*."

Mr. Brooke, the editor of the local newspaper, sometimes boarded his Great Dane at King Street Kennels and was always prepared to give the rescue center some publicity. A good story would sell more copies, too.

"Good idea, Em. I'll call him after breakfast," said her dad.

"Can't I do it?" said Emily.

Mr. Parker smiled and glanced at his wife. He knew how important this was for Emily. "Yes, I suppose so. Ask to speak to Mr. Brooke himself, though, and say you're from King Street Kennels."

Emily nodded and gulped down her breakfast

with an excited smile on her face. She couldn't wait to get her pet project moving. Sausage and Mash were absolutely adorable. She felt sure that half of Compton would want to offer them homes, once their cute faces appeared in the *News*.

Neil breezed into the kitchen then, pausing long enough at the table to make himself a jelly sandwich. "I'm just going to take a look at Jessie," he explained as he headed for the door, sandwich in hand.

"Neil! I'm going to call the newspaper about Sausage and Mash!" Emily called after him.

"Hey, that's great, Em!" His voice floated back through the door but he had already disappeared, with Sam slipping away silently after him.

Mrs. Parker sighed. "Mornings are like the bus station in this place," she complained. "Everybody zooming around, each going to a different destination."

It was true. But no matter what the rest of his family were up to, Neil's day always started with the dogs. They were the last thing he thought about each night when he fell asleep, and probably the first thing on his mind when he woke up.

As Neil walked across the courtyard toward the kennels he couldn't wait to see Jessie. There was something about that dog that made her stand out from the rest of their boarders. He couldn't put it into words, but it was something very special indeed, and he was determined to find out more about her.

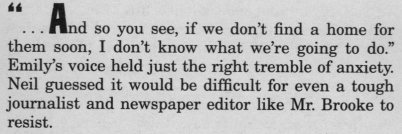

CHAPTER TWO

" **A**nd so you see, if we don't find a home for
them soon, I don't know what we're going to do."
Emily's voice held just the right tremble of anxiety.
Neil guessed it would be difficult for even a tough
journalist and newspaper editor like Mr. Brooke to
resist.

"This morning? Yes, yes, that'll be fine. Thanks
very much, Mr. Brooke." Emily put the phone down
and punched the air. "Yee-hah!" she yelled victori-
ously, her brown eyes shining. "Mr. Brooke's going to
send a photographer!"

There were cheers from the family.

"Good job, Emily," said her mom, laughing. "Maybe
you've got a career ahead of you as our Executive
Publicist."

Emily smoothed her dark brown hair. "We had to do something," she said. "Hardly anybody's come to the rescue center lately."

"We never get many people during the school holidays," Neil reminded her. "They're all away. That's why we've got so many boarders."

"But school holidays can also be the time when people abandon their pets," said their dad, "rather than pay for kennels while they go on vacation."

Neil looked down at Sam, remembering how they had rescued him when *he* was a puppy. Some people could be unbelievably cruel to their animals, and it made him so angry.

"Well," said Carole Parker, sensing that they were all becoming a little gloomy, "let's see what Emily's publicity does for Sausage and Mash. With any luck we can persuade the paper to give us another plug for the work we do at the center and — who knows? — we could get trampled in the rush of people coming to offer them good homes."

"Is anyone going to do any work today," asked Emily, "or am I on my own? We need to get the place looking respectable for the photographer!"

"Yes, ma'am. Right away, ma'am!" Bob said, pretending to touch a nonexistent cap. "Maybe you ought to be Head Foreman, too!"

Outside, the pale, clear sky and apricot rays of early sunshine promised a beautiful autumn day. The racket coming from the kennels told Neil that Kate McGuire, their kennel assistant, was already at work. The boarders sounded excitable, anticipating their breakfast.

"Morning, Kate!" Neil called as he made his way down the line of pens.

"Hi, Neil." Kate strode toward him, grinning broadly, carrying a couple of food bowls. She was wearing jeans and a sweatshirt, and her long blond hair was swept up in a messy ponytail. "You helping out again today?"

Neil looked at his watch. "Yeah, later on, anyway. I'm taking Sam out first."

"Oh, who's this?" Kate stopped at Jessie's pen, putting the bowl on the floor so she could squat down to talk to her. "Hello, sweetheart. We haven't seen you before, have we?"

"This is Jessie." Neil told her all about Mr. Harding and his after-hours visit the previous night. "Apparently she's expecting puppies in three weeks," he informed Kate, who was stroking and admiring Jessie.

"Oh?" Kate peered closely at Jessie. "She doesn't look very pregnant, but dogs do carry their puppies quite high. They're tucked right up under the rib cage until the final week or so. Then the puppies drop lower down and get ready to be born. With Jessie, though, it's hard to see where her tummy stops and her hair begins!"

Neil laughed. He took Jessie's leash off the hook, went into her pen, and clipped it onto her collar. "I'd like to take her out with Sam," he said.

"Could you handle another two as well? We've got a lot to walk right now."

"OK. Any two?"

"How about Max and Flora, then you won't have too many big dogs to handle," said Kate mischievously.

"Since when was that a problem?" said Neil, indignant.

Kate grinned. "Just teasing, Neil!"

Neil pretended to aim a kick at her ankle and Kate danced away with the bowls, laughing.

"I'll just get rid of these," she called back to him, "and then I'll come out with you."

Neil left Jessie clipped to the door of the kennel while he went to round up the other two dogs. They were regular boarders and he knew them well: Flora was a rough-coated Jack Russell with heaps of personality, while Max was a rather overweight dachshund who thought only of eating and sleeping. He could certainly do with some exercise.

Kate soon collected four of the other dogs and joined Neil outside the kennel block in the courtyard. The excited dogs took some controlling, but Kate quelled them all with a single *"Quiet!"* delivered with so much authority that Neil fell silent for a few seconds, too.

With his three dogs trotting and padding beside him, Neil led the way to the gate leading out of the kennels' enclosure. He whistled for Sam.

As he had expected, a streak of black and white shot out from under the hedge — Sam's favorite place — and raced them all to the gate.

"Hey, way to go, Sam!" said Kate as he passed her.

They caught up with Sam as he sat expectantly by the gate, wagging his tail. This was his chance to show off to the others.

"Open the gate, Sam!" Neil commanded.

Right away, Sam leaped up to the latch and knocked it with his nose. The gate opened enough for him to push his way through and make a gap wide enough for them all.

Neil praised and patted the collie, then waited for Kate and her team to come through before pulling the gate shut behind them.

"You ought to train him to shut it as well, you know!" Kate laughed.

They continued around the edge of the field. Flora was pulling ahead, impatient to run, while Max, as usual, was lagging behind. Jessie was alert, but seemed content to keep pace with Neil. Sam, of course, ran freely, but came back frequently to circle around them all in sheepdog fashion and make sure they were keeping up.

Neil and Kate liked to let the dogs off their leashes if they could, as they all enjoyed a free run. But it took good judgment: Few dogs were trained to Sam's level of obedience, and once off the leash they could be uncontrollable. Flora, for instance, would disappear quickly down the first rabbit hole if she had the chance. Max, however, would flop down in the grass and wait for them to pick him up on the way back.

Kate had brought two elderly golden retrievers, Prince and Alfie, together with a young Irish setter named Macduff. She would have to keep a firm hold of Macduff, because he had a tendency to take off like a rocket and not come back. Neil expected her to let the others have a good run, though.

Walking briskly, Neil looked down at Jessie and wondered if he could trust her. She had been OK in the yard the previous night, but out in the fields was another matter entirely. Would she come back to him if he called her?

"Are you going to let Jessie have a run, Neil?" asked Kate, breaking into his thoughts.

"I was just wondering that," he said. "I'd like to try. She seems very well behaved."

Reaching the far side of the field, they all went through a second gate and began to walk up to the track that ran along the ridgeway. From there they would be able to see all over Compton and the surrounding countryside: patchwork fields, miniature farms, and toy cows. It was a terrific view.

Poor fat Max was finding the hill difficult to climb, so Neil was obliged to slow down for him while Kate went on ahead. With Sam dancing around them impatiently, Neil thought it might be a good time to let Jessie have some freedom.

He bent to release Jessie's leash. "Now don't let me down, Jess," he said. "I'm counting on you to be as good as Sam!"

Jessie looked up at him as if she understood. As soon as she was free, she ran over to Sam and they raced ahead together, chasing and sparring like playful puppies. Neil laughed as he watched them charging down the hill. Suddenly he realized they were heading for the river.

Oh, no! he thought. His mom would shoot him if he let Sam get covered in mud! He sent out a piercing whistle.

"Sam! Jessie! Here! Come, Sam!" he yelled.

Both dogs stopped. Jessie looked back uncertainly, but Sam ran back to Neil as if his life depended on it.

"Jessie!" Neil called again. "Come, Jess!"

This time she broke into an athletic trot, racing after Sam so that with her larger stride, she managed to arrive at Neil's feet at the same time as the collie.

"Good dogs!" Neil praised them, giving both a small treat from the packet he always carried in his jacket pocket, and making a big fuss over them.

He looked inquisitively at Jessie. Who could have trained her that well? Harding had said he lived in Compton. King Street Kennels ran the only dog obedience classes in the region. Jessie didn't look much more than two years old, and, from the affection between her and Harding, Neil felt sure she had been with him since she was a puppy. Either she was a natural wonder-dog, or she had been to a very good class somewhere else, and if so, Neil wanted to know where.

As the crest of the hill appeared, Neil saw Kate sitting on a large stone with Macduff at her side and the other dogs wandering freely around them.

"Are you OK?" Kate asked him.

"Yeah, of course. Did you see Jessie come back to me just then?"

"I did. You took a chance, though, didn't you? Suppose she hadn't come back?"

Neil thought he had better not tell her about the previous night's experiment. "I just knew she would," he grinned. "I was more worried about them both diving into the river. I'd love to see what she's like at retrieving. I bet she's great!"

"Come on, then," said Kate, getting up from her seat. "Let's find out." She called to her charges, who obediently trotted to her side and, with Sam leading, they all went down a narrow path that led to a small bunch of trees and bushes. Neil had often brought Sam here when he was training him: It was quiet, and away from distractions.

Once among the trees, Neil looped Max's and Flora's leashes over a branch. Kate tied Macduff and the two retrievers next to them.

"You puppies sit there for a while and watch," Neil said. "You might learn something!"

Max flopped down right away, glad to rest.

With Kate standing nearby, watching, Neil began to take Jessie through the routine of retrieving.

"Sit, Jessie!" he commanded. Jessie promptly sat on her haunches, watching him with interest. "Stay!"

Sam watched eagerly. He knew that a game was coming up. "Now, Sam, you're going to have to sit this one out," Neil told him. He ordered Sam to lie down and stay put. Then he looked around and found a good, fat stick.

"Here, Jessie. Take a good sniff of this." He showed it to Jessie, letting her sniff both the stick and his hands, then he turned and flung the stick as far as he could out of the grove. "Fetch, Jessie!"

The large brown dog took off after it. Her pregnancy didn't appear to affect the speed at which she could run and in no time at all she had returned with the stick in her mouth. She ran up to Neil, sat down in front of him, and waited, looking up at him with sparkling eyes.

"Give," said Neil. He tapped the side of his left leg.

Jessie immediately dropped the stick at his feet, then circled around him to sit closely at his side. It was as professional a performance as he had ever seen.

Kate laughed and clapped her hands, delighted.

"Atta girl, Jessie!" she cried. "That dog's got real showmanship, Neil!"

"Yep," Neil replied a bit absently. He was still puzzling over where Jessie had received such great training.

He was just about to ask Kate if she knew of any other dog trainers in the Compton area, when Macduff suddenly tugged his leash free of the tree branch it had been tied to and ran off, yelping with excitement.

"Oh, no!" groaned Kate.

Stunned, she and Neil watched as the scatter-brained setter ran full-speed down the hillside, his leash flapping along beside him, grass and stones flying out in all directions.

"It'll take forever for us to catch him." Kate sighed. "He's definitely not a well-trained dog. If only it was Max, instead!"

"Kate!" gasped Neil, gripping her arm. "The fence!"

Macduff was charging toward an electrified sheep-fence that stretched across the bottom end of the field.

"Here!" cried Kate, pushing the leash into Neil's hands. "I've got to stop him!" She sprinted after the dog as fast as she could.

Neil quickly gathered his wits in time to send Sam after her.

"Fetch them, Sam!" he commanded. "After them!"

The collie needed no persuading to veer away to the right, moving like lightning, as if to collect his straying sheep. Neil watched nervously.

Suddenly, a large, dark golden shape joined Kate as she ran, and quickly overtook her. It was Jessie. With powerful ease, she streaked after Macduff, purpose and discipline in each of her strides.

As Neil watched in disbelief, Jessie caught up with the runaway dog from behind and took his leash in her mouth. She brought the setter to an abrupt halt just in front of the electric fence.

Meekly, and looking rather bemused, Macduff

trotted beside Jessie as she tugged him back up the hill toward Kate and Neil. Sam ran back and forth behind them, making sure they were heading the right way.

"Neil, Neil!" gasped Kate when he caught up with her. "Did you see that? What a great idea of yours, sending Jessie after Macduff. How did you know it would work?"

"It had nothing to do with me," Neil admitted. "Jessie did it all on her own. When I sent Sam, she went, too."

"Wow," said Kate, still breathless from her run. "I've never seen anything like it. Who did you say her owner was?"

"A man named Harding," Neil replied. "He lives in

Compton but he had to go to Japan on a business trip."

"If he lives in Compton, then who trained Jessie? I don't know of anybody but us who trains dogs in such advanced stuff," said Kate. "I hope some rival hasn't started up classes . . ."

"Let's not say anything to my mom and dad about it," Neil said thoughtfully. "There's a mystery here and I want to be the one to solve it."

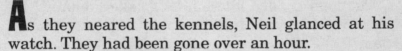

CHAPTER THREE

As they neared the kennels, Neil glanced at his watch. They had been gone over an hour.

"Oh, no!" he groaned. "I'd forgotten all about the photographer coming. I promised Emily I'd help clean up."

Once the dogs were safely back in their pens, Neil went to join his sister in the rescue center. Emily had done a good job of making the place look even cleaner and neater than usual — by herself. Neil tried to hide his guilty feelings by whistling as he walked up to join the group already assembled there.

Emily gave him a quick scowl before she turned back to the photographer, who was holding Mash and stroking him gently.

"You know, I'd take this little guy home myself, if I could," he said, trying to keep a firm grip on the warm, wriggling puppy.

"Should I try to persuade you?" asked Mrs. Parker as she came in behind Neil.

"No, it wouldn't be fair," the photographer said reluctantly, handing Mash back to Emily. "With this job, I'm hardly ever at home."

"Ah, what a pity," said Mrs. Parker.

The photographer was a young man with long hair tied back in a ponytail. Neil had recognized him immediately. "You're the man who took the photos at the County Show this year, aren't you?"

The man nodded and smiled. "Jake Fielding." He shook hands with Neil and his mother. "Where's Sam?"

"Probably under the hedge, sleeping off his walk," Neil grinned. "I'll see if he'll come and say hello."

Neil walked back to the door and whistled. In no time, Sam came hurtling into the rescue center and sat at Neil's feet, looking up at him expectantly.

Neil felt in his pocket for another treat.

The photographer knelt down to stroke him. "You're a beauty, Sam. I wish I had a dog like you."

Sam enjoyed all the fuss. He nosed in the photographer's pocket to see if he had any treats. Everybody laughed.

"Now then," the photographer said, getting to his feet once more. He took out a battered shorthand notebook. "Tell me all about Sausage and Mash here, and who's been looking after them. Great names, by the way."

Emily stepped forward. Now that her moment had arrived, she suddenly felt rather shy. She held a squirming brown-and-cream puppy in each hand while she gave Jake their story.

"Any idea what breed they might be?" Jake asked.

"Quite mixed, I'm afraid," said Mrs. Parker. "Could be some boxer, and maybe some Staffordshire bull terrier. They're bound to be tough, smooth-coated, friendly, and with plenty of character, though!"

Jake laughed. "Well, you certainly know your dogs, Mrs. Parker!"

"We see them all here," said Emily. "In fact,

pedigree dogs are just as likely to need rescuing as mongrels."

"Is that right?" said the photographer. "You'd think that if people spend a lot of money on a dog they'd be sure to look after it."

"Well, sometimes they grow bigger than people expect. And they have to be exercised every day," Emily told him. "Or they might need expensive medical treatment."

"What a rotten thing to do, abandoning your dog when it's sick and needs you most!" the photographer burst out.

Mrs. Parker reached out and took one of the puppies from Emily. "My guess is that these arrived unexpectedly — maybe the mother was a pedigree Staffordshire and this litter was something of an embarrassment to her owner. In any event, they aren't valuable enough to sell for a decent price."

Jake studied the puppies thoughtfully. "Well, I think it's a real shame. Anyway . . ." He picked up his camera and quickly checked the light meter. "Let's get a close-up of you, Emily, with a puppy in each hand. Hold them near your face, one on either side. That's right. Lots of sentimental appeal to ooze off the page at our readers! Come on, puppies, give us a smile!"

Emily laughed and one of the pups licked her face just as the flash went off.

"Great! And again!"

Jake took lots of photographs from different angles. The puppies wriggled and squirmed, wanting to get down to play, while Emily beamed into the lens.

"There — that should do it," said Jake. He rewound the film and removed it from his camera. Quickly writing something on the label, he popped it into one of his many baggy pockets.

"By the way, I'd better ask which one's which," Jake said.

Neil took one of the pups from his sister. "They look so much alike, I'm not sure myself," he confessed.

"That's Mash!" Emily informed him crossly. "Can't you tell by now? He's got three white paws and one brown one, and Sausage has got four white ones. If you spent as much time with them as *I* do, you'd —"

Just then Bob Parker called through the doorway and interrupted the argument that was brewing.

"Neil! When you've finished up here, Kate could use a hand," he said, and disappeared again.

"OK, Dad." He handed Mash back to Emily and then excused himself, saying that he looked forward to seeing Jake's story in the *News*.

Neil found Kate in Kennel Block One.

"We've got four dogs going home and four new ones arriving today," said Kate. "I'll need some help scrubbing out the pens."

Neil nodded. Not the best job in the kennels, he thought.

"Two pens each," said Kate. "I'll go into Block Two, and you can stay in here if you like. Oh, and you might take a look at our heroine. After all that running around she seems to have tired out. I haven't forgotten about what you said, by the way. I'll ask around, see if anyone's heard of another trainer. Did Harding say how long he's lived in Compton?"

Neil shook his head. "No, just that he lived at one-forty-nine Dale End Road. I checked the address on his card in the office."

"Hmm." Kate pursed her lips, thinking hard, but said no more on the subject. She promised to try and see him later and check to see how clean the pens were.

Jessie was sleeping, her head on her front paws. Unlike the other dogs, Jessie seemed like a slow and dainty eater. Despite the energy she had used up earlier, she had only finished about half of her food.

Neil picked up a brush and started attacking the empty pen. He hoped she would be OK.

Jessie still hadn't eaten much food when it was time for the kennels to be closed up for the night. Neil was helping his mother with the routine locking-up and pointed it out.

"Should I take this away and give her some fresh food?" he asked.

"I don't think there's much point," said Carole Parker. "She's obviously quite healthy. Some dogs eat a lot when they're expecting, and some stop eating. We have to let them tell us what they want. Maybe we should let Jessie take it easy tomorrow. Just a stroll around the yard, not a marathon trek like the one you took her on today."

"Fine. I was planning to go over to Chris's tomorrow anyway, so it's OK with me not to have to take any of them for a long walk." Chris Wilson was Neil's best friend from school. "He's going to show me his new bike. Wish *I* had a new one, Mom . . ."

"You'd better start thinking of ways to earn one, then." Carole Parker glanced around the courtyard. "The kennels will be due for a new coat of paint soon."

"Oh, Mom!" Neil groaned. His old bike, which was feeling slightly small for him these days, would just have to last a while longer.

CHAPTER FOUR

Tuesday was a rainy day and nobody was in a good mood. Even the dogs seemed miserable. Sam was sprawled out on the doormat with his head on his paws. He looked as if he wanted to go for a walk, but every time the door was opened, he shrank back, tail between his legs, as a flurry of rain blew in.

The kennels were a dismal place to be. Despite having playthings, comfortable quarters, and plenty to eat, every dog seemed to be moping and scowling. Neil's and Emily's attempts to get Max the dachshund out for a walk had failed. He had simply splayed out his paws and, after having dragged him a few inches with his claws rasping on the floor of his pen, they had given up and let that particular sleeping dog lie.

Neil was in his bedroom, idly flicking through a football magazine but not really reading it.

"What's up with you?" asked Emily, breezing in and plonking herself down at the end of his bed with a bounce.

"I keep thinking about Jessie. I can't get her off my mind."

"That brown dog who rescued Macduff?"

"Yes," said Neil. "*That* brown dog. I think she's the most intelligent, talented dog we've ever had here, you know. She's only staying for a week, but I want to find out everything she can do."

"Isn't she having puppies?" Emily asked. "Do you think she'll have them while she's with us?"

"I'm afraid not. She's not due for another two and a half weeks and Mr. Harding's picking her up on Friday."

"That man!" Emily's lips pursed.

"What do you mean?"

"I think I agree with Sarah that he's weird."

"Sarah couldn't have said that," Neil pointed out.

"No. 'Funny' is what she said."

"Anyway, what do you know? I saw him and he was perfectly normal. There was a real bond between him and Jessie. *You* didn't even see him," Neil reminded her. "You were glued to the TV."

Emily shrugged and nodded. "I've still got this . . . *feeling* about him, though," she said.

"You can't believe Sarah — she's only a baby!" scoffed Neil.

"Let's see this wonderful Jessie of yours," said Emily, changing the subject before they started arguing. It seemed everybody was arguing with everybody else today. In the house, their parents were fighting over what color to paint the kennels. Carole Parker preferred green, while Bob said that white was more hygienic and clean-looking. Sarah was in her most demanding mode, requiring everybody to find things for her. So Emily was grateful for a chance to slip out to the kennels with her brother.

They came to Jessie's pen. She immediately sat up and thumped her tail.

"Looks like she wants to go for a walk," Emily observed.

"You could be right. Let's just take her as far as the field, though. I don't want to wear her out. Or me," Neil said.

Sam appeared as they clipped on Jessie's leash, and waited to be allowed to open the gate. Once in the field, Neil let Jessie off her leash. He demonstrated her skills at sitting and staying and Emily threw a ball for her to retrieve.

"This is really easy for her," he said. "She's capable of much more."

His sister had a sudden idea. "I wonder if she can tell left from right?"

"You try," Neil suggested.

Emily threw the ball for Jessie, then asked her to stay. She obeyed. Then Emily yelled, "Right, Jessie. Go right," while gesturing with her right hand.

To their amazement, Jessie loped off to the right-hand hedge, where she stopped and looked at them questioningly.

"OK, Jessie. Left, left!" Emily shouted, this time pointing with her left hand. Jessie trotted over to the opposite hedge, then sank down, waiting for her next instruction.

Emily's face was animated. "This is incredible!

Look what I'm going to try now," she said. "Around, Jessie. Around in a circle!" She drew a circle in the air with her fingers. Jessie hesitated for a moment, as if this was something she dimly remembered but hadn't done for ages, then she trotted around in a tight, neat circle and sat down again.

Emily ran over to her and gave her a pat and a stroke. "Good girl. Clever girl!" she praised her and gave her a doggy treat from Neil's packet. "She must have had a really good trainer, Neil. Don't you think?" Emily commented.

Neil raised his eyebrows and grunted. He and Kate were already on this particular case, and what he had just seen Jessie do made him even more determined to crack it.

The following morning, the trees and grass sparkled with raindrops but the rain had stopped. Neil had promised Chris that they would go for a long bike ride if it was dry out. Before he set off, Neil made his usual breakfast visit to see how the dogs were doing.

Fat Max was going home that day. "I'm going to give his owners a diet plan. It's disgusting, letting a dog get into that state," Kate said.

"You wait till you see them," Neil chuckled. "I was here when they brought him in. Ever hear that owners look like their pets?"

Neil gave Max a scratch on his big, fat belly. He

peered into Jessie's pen across the way and sighed. The dog was sleeping and looked very peaceful.

"By the way, I made some inquiries yesterday," Kate told him. "About Harding. I called up all my friends with dogs and, aside from that place over at Stackbridge — you know, the place run by that awful woman who breeds chihuahuas — nobody knows of anyone running training and obedience classes within twenty miles. That's why they all come here."

Neil frowned. "So Jessie must have been trained somewhere other than Compton," he said. "I wonder how long Mr. Harding has been living here?"

"Never, by the look of things," Kate said. She smiled triumphantly.

"What on earth do you mean?"

"My friend Jane lives on Dale End Road — at number one-thirty-nine. The last house is number one-forty-seven. Harding told us he lived at one-forty-nine. Well, that house doesn't even exist!"

"Phew, this is tough going, isn't it?" Neil complained, wiping the back of his hand across his forehead as he and Chris stopped their bikes. They were halfway to the ridge.

They had started off by following the route Neil and Kate had taken with the dogs two days earlier. Then, in order to give Chris's new bike the tough test that he wanted, they had left the track and plunged into the patch of woodland that grew thickly on one side. Neil, with his older, narrower tires and fewer gears, puffed in Chris's wake. Whereas Chris's bike bounded over tree roots and tufts of grass, Neil's kept lurching to a halt, almost hurling him over the handlebars more than once.

Despite the weather and the fact that it was a half-term vacation, they hadn't seen one other cyclist or walker on this particular part of the hill.

"Shh." Chris held up his hand as Neil opened his mouth to say something. "Listen . . ."

"To what?"

"The silence."

"You can't listen to silence, dummy. You can only listen to sounds."

"What's that?"

Both boys held their breath, tense with concentration.

"I can't hear a thing," Neil said.

"Shh!" ordered Chris.

After what seemed like an endless wait, Neil got fed up. "It was a blackbird," he snorted.

"I didn't mean the bird. There was definitely something else. It was a sort of whimpering sound, like an animal in pain," insisted Chris.

"There are plenty of foxes around here," Neil pointed out.

"It didn't sound like a fox. Maybe something's fallen and hurt itself. Maybe we should take a look around," said Chris.

"OK, but not for too much longer. We've got a big food delivery on the way and I promised Mom I'd be back by one."

They dragged and bounced their bikes over roots and stones, across ditches and under branches, but failed to see or hear anything out of the ordinary. In the end, they had to head for home.

Christ didn't ride all the way with Neil. After coming through the field, he stopped by the first gate. "I think my gears need work. I'm going to take them apart here. You go on," he said. "See you."

"Yeah. Tomorrow?"

"OK," Chris agreed.

The two of them met again much sooner than they had intended. It was about ten after three that afternoon and Neil was helping to unload boxes of dog food from the delivery van and put them away in the pantry, when he heard Chris call his name. There was something strange about his voice — an urgency — that told him instantly that something was wrong.

Telling his dad that he'd be back in a moment, he raced over to the main gate, where Chris was waiting for him. Instead of sitting on his bike, Chris was standing beside it and his right arm was stretched awkwardly between the handle and the seat.

As Neil drew nearer, he could see that a makeshift

stretcher, constructed from branches, had been held together with Chris's belt and the cable from his bike lock. On it lay a dark, still shape.

A cold, creepy sensation washed over Neil. He felt slightly sick. "What is it?" he called over to his friend.

"A dog. He's in very bad shape."

CHAPTER FIVE

"**D**ad. *Dad!*" yelled Neil. "Come here, quick!"

Gently, they lifted the heavy, unconscious animal down from the bike. Then Chris leaned the bike against the fence and attempted to rub some life back into his numb arm. He had been carefully holding the homemade stretcher in position for almost half an hour.

"Where did you find him?" Neil asked, watching as his father quickly assessed the situation and took the dog into the treatment room.

"I was back up on the ridge. I heard the sound again and managed to figure out where it was coming from. I found him lying in a shallow stream. I think he tried to get a drink and collapsed."

"Let's go and see how he is."

The dog was lying on the examination table. From the shape of his ears and muzzle, and the deep brown and black color of his coat, he looked, to Neil's experienced eyes, to be some kind of Doberman cross.

Bob Parker was on the phone to the vet. "Bad wound to his back leg, Mike," he was saying. "And one of his eyes is badly swollen. It looks as if he's been hit by something."

Mike Turner was an old friend of the Parkers and a frequent visitor. He said he would come over right away.

The injured dog stirred. He made a feeble attempt

to lift his head. It looked almost too heavy for his neck to support.

"You don't think he's broken any bones in his neck or back, do you?" Neil asked his father.

"Don't think so. He wouldn't be able to move his head at all if that were the case."

Bob Parker placed a tin bowl of water in front of the dog. He appeared to want it, but didn't have the strength to lap, so Neil fetched a dropper and dripped some water into the dog's mouth.

"Shouldn't you give him some food as well? He might be starving to death!" asked Chris.

"Not until the vet has seen him. We don't know what this guy has been through. He might have internal injuries," Bob said.

Neil put a blanket over the dog, who was shivering.

When Mike Turner arrived, he gave the dog an expert examination and announced that it had multiple abrasions and four broken ribs.

"It looks as if he might have been kicked or beaten," he said grimly. "They're new injuries. You can tell by the color of the bruise around his eye. It can't be more than twenty-four hours old. It's this wound on his leg that's done most of the damage, though. See here?"

Mike parted the blood-matted fur. They saw the deep gouge carved in the animal's back leg. "I can't tell what has caused it. It's not a knife wound —

wrong shape. But it's shattered the bone right here, and nicked a vein. He's probably lost quite a lot of blood."

"Lying in the water won't have helped," said Neil.

"No. He may be suffering from hypothermia. The water's probably freezing." The vet turned to Chris. "Where exactly was the spot where you found him?"

"In the woods near the ridge."

"Well, you do get poachers going up there, shooting wood pigeons and rabbits. It could be a bullet wound, I suppose," Mike said. "That would have caused this clean, deep cut. But I don't know how he could have sustained the other injuries, unless he was abused."

Mike stopped and frowned. He looked at the dog on the table again. "No, he's quite well fed and looks as if he was in good shape until this happened."

"I wonder why nobody's reported him missing?" said Chris.

"I don't know," said Mr. Parker. "We'll report all this to the police, of course."

"You do that, Bob," said Mike. "Meanwhile, I'm going to take him to the intensive care unit and see what I can do for him."

"Will he be OK?" asked Neil.

Mike shrugged. "It's touch and go. He's in shock. The sudden blood loss hasn't helped, either."

"We know you'll do your best, Mike," said Mr. Parker. "Keep us posted, won't you?"

"Sure thing," Mike promised. "Give him twenty-four hours, and then you can come and see him." He paused and added, "We'll need a name for him."

"I think we should call him Soldier," said Chris, "because he's been so brave."

There was no disagreement.

"OK. Soldier it is."

After Mike Turner had left, Bob Parker turned to Neil and Chris. "The best thing you two can do now is get involved in something else. No sense in worrying too much about Soldier — Mike will let us know soon enough if he's going to make it or not."

Neil nodded, but he was still upset.

"I'd better be going," announced Chris, looking at his watch.

Neil walked him to the front gate.

"You OK, buddy?" asked Neil, sensing his friend was still shaken up by the afternoon's events.

"Just about. Will you let me know if you hear any more from the vet, or if you find his owner?"

"You'll be the first to know," Neil promised.

"I think I might go up there again. See if I can find any cartridge shells."

"Careful you don't get hit yourself," said Neil.

"Poachers usually operate at night. I'll be all right. Anyway, I'm a little bigger than a pigeon or a dog. They couldn't miss me."

"That's just what I'm worried about!" said Neil.

Then his voice was serious again. "I'll go to the vet's tomorrow. You coming?"

"You bet!" said Chris.

The mood in King Street Kennels the next morning was somber. Everyone had heard about Soldier and although work went on as normal, there was a tense atmosphere of expectancy as they waited to hear from Mike Turner.

Chris was at the back door just as Neil was finishing his breakfast. "Any news about Soldier yet?"

"No, nothing — it's early, though," Neil told him. "I'm just going to check on Jessie. Want to come?"

"Can I come, too?" Sarah squeaked excitedly.

"Oh, please take her with you," Carole begged them. "I've got loads to do and she's really a handful this morning."

"OK," Neil agreed, reluctantly. Why did he have to put up with a kid sister hanging around? Chris was grinning at him, enjoying Neil's frustration.

Kate was out with some of the dogs when they got to the kennel block. They found Jessie lying in a corner of her pen, looking rather bored.

"Can I pet her?" Sarah asked them.

"Of course you can," said Neil, opening the pen.

The big, gentle dog thumped her tail as Sarah stroked her head very gently.

"What's this?" Chris inquired, pointing to a piece of folded paper poked through the wire of Jessie's pen.

Neil pulled it out. It was from Kate, addressed to him.

He read it aloud: "*I think Sam's feeling a little neglected. Why don't you give him some training exercises today?*"

"Can I come and watch?" begged an eager voice from Jessie's pen. "*Please.* I won't get in the way! I promise!"

"But you always do —" Neil began.

"She'll be OK," said Chris. "I can keep an eye on her while you work the dogs."

Neil raised his eyes in mock despair. "It's a conspiracy! Come on. We'll take Jessie, too."

While Sarah sat on a bench, stroking the two dogs, Neil and Chris struggled out onto the field, carrying old tires, planks, a barrel, and some balls. They made several trips before Neil was satisfied. "This should do," he said at last.

Sam was getting very excited, fidgeting in his place. Even Jessie had her ears pricked up with interest.

Neil and Chris then built the runs, put up posts for the dogs to weave through, erected planks for them to run along, tires to squeeze through, and a length of wood balanced over some bricks to make a seesaw.

Once it was finished, Chris flopped onto the bench next to Sarah, wiping his brow.

Neil called Sam. Immediately, he rose from his place beside Sarah and came over to him.

"Good boy!" Neil said. He looked over at Jessie. "And let's see what you make of all this, Jess."

Neil led Sam to the start of the Agility course. He could sense Jessie watching them expectantly, all her senses alert. She made a move to follow Sam.

"No, Jess. You can't do it," he said. "We don't want you to fall off anything. You might hurt your puppies."

Jessie's reaction was a sharp, impatient bark and a whine, as if she were saying, "Go on, let me."

Neil remembered his mother saying that pregnant dogs knew how much food and exercise they wanted, and you had to let them tell you. Jessie was a sensible, intelligent dog. She wouldn't put her puppies at risk. If there was a jump or an activity she wasn't capable of doing, she simply wouldn't do it.

"OK — go, Jess, go!" he commanded, and held onto Sam's collar as a precaution.

To Neil's delighted surprise, Jessie bounded over and leaped onto the first plank. Then she ran swiftly, negotiating each obstacle as if she'd been doing it all her life. She flew through the tires without hesitating, and only slowed down for the rather wobbly seesaw. She completed the course quickly and without a fault, finishing by sitting at Neil's feet.

"That's incredible," said Chris. "She's done this before, right?"

"This dog gets more amazing by the minute," Neil replied, grinning proudly as he rubbed her head.

"Now it's Sam's turn," Chris said.

Neil was idly looking around the exercise field. "Hang on. Where's Sarah?"

Chris looked around, too. There was no sign of her.

"She can't have gone far." Chris felt rather uneasy. He had promised to keep an eye on Sarah, but he'd been busy watching Jessie's performance. "Come on," said Chris. "Let's go and find her. I bet she's playing hide-and-seek."

"Wait, maybe Sam can show us where she is," said Neil. "Look, there's Sarah's hanky." He picked up the scrap of material from the bench and then held Sam still while he wrapped it loosely around the dog's nose. "Fetch, Sam. Fetch Sarah."

Sam bounded around Neil, barking excitedly. But his eyes were watching the hanky, to see if Neil was going to throw it for him.

"It's no good," said Neil. "He hasn't been trained to track people. He doesn't know what I want."

They called Sarah's name loudly, but she didn't appear.

"How about Jessie?" Chris suggested.

Neil looked down at the shaggy dog sitting patiently by his side. You never know, he thought. She just might be trained to do this, too.

"OK," said Neil, "We'll give it a try. You'll have to hold onto Sam for me, Chris."

Neil draped Sarah's handkerchief over Jessie's nose.

Jessie sniffed it with interest.

"Find Sarah, Jessie. Where's Sarah? Find her!"

Jessie looked up at Neil once, then bounded away with her graceful lope. She seemed to know exactly where she was going, her nose down near the ground as she followed the scent left by Neil's sister.

The boys ran behind, restraining Sam, who was eager to join in this new game, and trying hard to keep Jessie in sight. She disappeared into a thick clump of trees and bushes at the far end of the field, and they heard her bark once.

Sam barked in reply, eager to follow.

Neil and Chris scratched and scraped their way through a tunnel of brambles. There, in the center of her new den, they found Sarah, sitting on a moss-covered tree root with her arm around Jessie, grinning delightedly. Sam barged in, too, and started licking her face.

"Oh, Sam, stop!" she cried.

"Sarah, how could you run off like that? You scared us to death!" said Neil. "We had to ask Jessie to find you."

Sarah gave a giggle. "I like playing hide-and-seek," she said. "Can we play it again?"

"No, we definitely can't!" said Neil, angrily. "Come on, you're going back to the house."

"Jessie was pretty fantastic, Neil," said Chris, brushing himself down once they were all out in the open field again. "Shouldn't you give her a biscuit, or something?"

Jessie's head cocked to one side and her tail began to wag.

Neil smiled in spite of being so mad about Sarah's game.

"Here, Jess!" he called.

Jessie needed no second prompting. She ran over to Neil's feet, sat rigidly, and watched his every move as he put his hand into his pocket.

"Good girl, Jess. You were wonderful!"

"Look at Sam!" squealed Sarah.

Sam was sitting up on his haunches, waving both front paws in the air at Neil and making pathetic little whines.

"Jeez, Sam," said Neil. "When did you learn that little number?"

"I think he just taught himself!" gasped Chris, chuckling with laughter.

"Jessie's done it again though, hasn't she?" said Neil.

"Done what?"

"Something totally unexpected. She keeps showing off different bits of her training. If she were a different breed, I'd say she'd been trained as a police dog."

"Hey, you don't think Harding's really a policeman, do you?" said Chris.

"I'll have to ask him when he comes to pick her up. You know, you could have something there. If he were a detective working on a big case, he might not want anyone to know his real address." Neil had told Chris about the phantom 149 Dale End Road.

"Yes, but surely a policeman would know you might have to check out his address? It doesn't make sense. . . ."

"No, it doesn't," Neil agreed. "C'mon, let's put all the stuff back in the pantry and get Sarah back inside. There might be some news about Soldier."

CHAPTER SIX

They returned to the house to find everybody crowded around the big wooden table in the Parkers' kitchen. Bob had just got back from town with an early edition of the *Compton News* and a bag of doughnuts.

The paper was spread out on the table, surrounded by mugs of hot tea.

Sarah scrambled up onto a chair to get a better view.

The headline leaped out from a corner of the third page. Underneath the banner was the photograph of Emily, with the puppies by each side of her face staring appealingly into the camera. It was perfect.

"Sausage and Mash in desperate bid to find home," read Bob Parker.

Emily's face was pink with pleasure. "It's good, isn't it?" she said.

"Terrific," said her father.

"Great," her mother agreed. "We should ask them for a copy of that picture."

"Not bad, Em. But don't give up the day job," said Neil.

Emily dug him in the ribs with her elbow.

"What does the story say?" asked Chris, leaning over Mr. Parker's back, trying to read. It was rather difficult with everyone moving the paper so that they could get a better look.

Bob Parker read the article out loud.

"Could you abandon two little puppies like these? Well, somebody did! Sausage and Mash, seen here with nine-year-old Emily Parker, were found abandoned, cold, and almost starved to death near the old railroad station in Compton. Now they desperately need homes. If you can help, call King Street Kennels and Rescue Center. And they've put our number in."

"Well, if that doesn't generate some interest, I don't know what will," said Carole Parker.

Bob closed the newspaper. "Better stand back, Em, or you'll be flattened in the rush."

"Look, Bob, there's been another antiques robbery, in one of those big houses in Aston this time," Carole said, indicating the main headline. "Wasn't a shop in Leigh robbed, too?"

"It's the first I've heard about it," said Neil.

"Where have you been, Neil?" said Mrs. Parker. "The last few months have been full of stories about thefts from homes and antiques shops. The police think it's one gang, possibly organized by a mastermind."

"Making it the biggest crime wave around here for years!" Chris added knowledgeably.

Neil was surprised. "Why are you so interested?"

"My dad's friend's shop in Padsham was robbed last month," said Chris. "They took all the really good stuff. Worth about a hundred grand."

"A hundred thousand dollars?" Neil was stunned. "If they took that much every time, they must be making a fortune."

Just then the phone rang. Mrs. Parker answered.

"It's someone who wants to come and see Sausage and Mash," she said as she put the phone down.

"The first call of many, I bet," said Bob Parker. "We'd better get ready for the deluge."

"Has Soldier's owner reported him missing yet?" Neil asked his dad.

"I spoke to Sergeant Moorhead this morning. They've checked the missing dog lists but nobody's lost one resembling Soldier."

"It's very strange. He was well fed, so he couldn't be a stray. Do you think he could have belonged to a poacher and they don't want to claim him in case the police find out about them?"

"It's possible."

"Some rotten person might have thrown him out of a car. People do that sometimes, don't they?" said Emily.

The phone rang again.

"I think we'll find homes for those two bundles of mischief in no time!" said Mr. Parker.

"I know!" said Emily, excitedly. "Why don't we get the paper to do an article on Soldier? Then we might find out who owns him."

"Worth a try, Em," said her dad. Then his face clouded over. "But I think we'd better wait and see if he recovers first."

Leaving Mrs. Parker and Emily to cope with the phone calls, Mr. Parker and Neil went off to check on the dogs. Chris mounted his bike, waved good-bye, and headed home.

"How's Jessie today?" Mr. Parker asked.

"If you'd seen the way she went around Sam's obstacle course, you wouldn't need to ask," Neil said proudly.

Realizing he might have got himself in trouble, Neil quickly changed the subject. Boarders, particularly pregnant ones, weren't supposed to risk life and limb on Sam's training course. "I think she's missing her owner, though. She gets a bit depressed and whimpery sometimes. Have you heard from him?"

"No, but there's a ten-hour time difference between here and Japan. It's probably very difficult for him to call. He's due back tomorrow, anyway. And we don't need to worry about her puppies — they're not due yet. Puppies are never more than three days early or late, unless there's something wrong."

Emily came running up from the direction of the house.

"I had to find you," she said breathlessly. "Guess what? We've got fourteen people who want to come and see the puppies!"

"Fourteen? That's fantastic!"

"But we've only got two puppies!" Emily looked anxious.

"I wouldn't panic," said Mr. Parker reassuringly. "Not everyone's going to be suitable. We probably won't need to see them all."

"I just hope we don't choose whoever had Soldier."

Neil gazed at his sister. The possibility of Soldier's owners coming to claim one of Emily's two homeless puppies had never occurred to him.

There were only two people left in the vet's waiting room in Compton when Neil and Chris arrived that evening. Janice, the nurse, said they could go straight through to the intensive care unit and see Soldier. She warned them to be very quiet though, so as not to excite the other animals too much.

The ICU section was a part of the hospital that Neil and Chris had never seen before. The place was spotless, with gleaming shelves, glass-covered cabinets, and shiny emergency equipment. The patients here, though, were in individual cages, lying on sheepskin or special heated mats.

They would have missed Soldier if Janice hadn't pointed him out to them. With his injured leg shaved and splinted and an IV taped to his left foreleg, he looked utterly helpless. A small label at the top of the cage identified him and gave details about his date of admission and treatment.

"He's still very weak," Janice told them. "We've done all we can for him, but he's definitely got a touch of pneumonia, too."

"That sounds bad," said Neil worriedly.

"It's not good. Normally we'd expect antibiotics to clear it up, but after the shock, and the loss of so much blood, he may not be strong enough to survive the infection." She paused. "Only time will tell."

After a few minutes of staring at Soldier and willing him to get better, they left the animal hospital, thanked Janice for her help, and mounted their bikes to ride home in the gathering gloom of the autumn evening.

On their way, they stopped outside the window of the video shop, which was having a sale.

"I've been thinking," Neil said as they gazed at the display. "You know our theory about Mr. Harding being an undercover policeman? You don't think he could be trying to find the antiques robbers, do you?"

Chris looked thoughtful. Then he said, "No, he can't be. Why put Jessie in the kennels for exactly a week? How would he know that it would take only a week to catch them? It doesn't make sense. Anyway, I've been thinking, too. If he's only just moved here, he could have got mixed up with Dale End Drive, around the corner. That goes up to one-sixty-one — I checked."

"I suppose so," said Neil. "You're probably right."

"By the way," Chris said, "I was up in the woods again today. I didn't find anything, though."

"Soldier might have run quite a long way from where he was injured. He must have been so scared. He probably just bolted."

"But there must be something we can do. Hey, what's going on?"

Neil spun around and saw a van careening erratically down the street toward them.

"The driver must be drunk!" said Chris.

The van was lurching from one side of the road to the other, but it looked too deliberate for the vehicle to be out of control.

"There's a car chasing it. Look!"

Neil spotted the black BMW that Chris had seen first. It was close behind the van.

"Quick! Get in the doorway!" Neil shouted urgently as the van headed in their direction.

They ducked into the shop doorway just in time. The van, with what looked like a redheaded driver at the wheel, mounted the pavement right where they had been standing, just missed a lamppost, then shot off down a side street.

"He's going to kill somebody!" Chris said.

The BMW couldn't make the quick right-hand turn. It missed the entrance to the narrow lane and continued on down the road. Neil felt sure he'd seen three men in it — two in the front and one in the back.

Shaken, Neil and Chris stepped out of the doorway.

"Are you OK?" Chris asked.

"Yeah. I wish I'd got their license plate numbers so

that we could have reported them. What do you think was going on?"

"I don't know. It looked like the BMW was chasing the van and the van driver was trying to shake it off."

"Well, it worked. He got rid of them, didn't he?" Neil said.

"But why was the car chasing the van?" Chris wondered.

Neil shrugged. "Maybe it was Compton's first example of road rage. Maybe the van cut off the BMW at the traffic light."

"It looked a bit more serious than that to me," Chris said. "That van driver looked as if he was scared to death!"

"Maybe he'd done something dreadful, like robbing a bank   "

"Maybe he owed money to the guys in the BMW —"

"Maybe it was a drug thing . . ."

Their speculations ground to a halt, though the imaginations of both boys were working overtime as they slowly rode home.

CHAPTER SEVEN

Neil had meant to tell his parents about the car chase, but other events soon put it out of his mind.

"Whose car is in the driveway, Mom?"

Neil threw his jacket on the banister and he and Chris joined Mrs. Parker in the kitchen.

"Honestly, Neil, you wouldn't believe how many people have been here to see Sausage and Mash." Carole Parker looked harassed as she sorted through some papers on the table.

"That's great! Wish we'd got back earlier. I might have been able to help out," said Neil.

"I had to leave your father and Emily sorting through them all. If it was up to Emily, though, I don't think we'd ever find homes for them! She has doubts about everyone. She keeps thinking about Soldier, I suppose. How is he?"

"Not so good. I could do some real damage to the person who did this to him!" Neil's threat was tinged with anger.

"This group seems really nice." Carole tried to counter his high emotions with some good news. "It's going to be hard to choose between them, but I think Emily has settled on someone just now. That's their car outside."

Crossing to the rescue center, Neil and Chris found Mr. Parker and Emily saying good-bye to a girl and a boy, both about ten years old, and their parents. The younger girl was carefully carrying a wriggling Mash.

"Have both puppies gone now?" Neil asked his sister as the family drove away.

"Yes," said Emily, quietly. "It's awful. I miss them already. Dad's told them he'll come by in a week to make sure everything's OK."

"Well, at least you got what you wanted, Em. Good homes for them both," said her dad. "That's what we're all about."

"Do you always do that?" asked Chris. "Check up, I mean."

"Oh, yes," Mr. Parker replied. "You have to make sure that the dog is happy and that the new owners aren't having second thoughts. If there are any doubts at all, we'd rather bring the dog back." He turned to Neil. "Have you looked in on Jessie today?"

"Not yet. I haven't had a chance. Heard from Mr. Harding yet?"

"Nope. I'm sure he'll call as soon as he's home, though. He must be missing her by now. You saw the bond between them."

"Mm-hmm," Neil agreed.

"He might be wrong about when those pups are due, though. Her tummy looks bulgy today. That doesn't normally happen till the eighth week. As you know, pregnancies are about nine weeks in all — sixty-three days."

"He'll be taking her home just in time, then."

"Looks like it."

At that moment, Neil's mother came running out of the office toward them, a stricken look on her face. "Mike Turner just called. He says Soldier isn't going to last through the day."

"Oh, no!" Chris let out a cry.

"I thought you might want Dad to take you back down there."

Neil and Chris exchanged glances and ran toward the house. Emily looked at her mother then ran after them.

"It's the pneumonia, I'm afraid," Mike Turner explained when they arrived at the animal hospital.

"We've done all we can but he's too weak to fight it. Poor guy."

"He doesn't have much time left, then?" asked Neil.

"No. 'Fraid not. I'll leave you with him. I'll be in the office with your dad."

As they pushed through the double doors into the intensive care unit, they could see Soldier lying in his special cage. The dog's shallow, fast, rasping breaths were painful to hear.

"Oh, Neil . . ." Emily didn't know what to say.

Neil put his arm around his sister's shoulders and gave her a comforting hug.

Chris stroked Soldier's silky head. "I was hoping I'd saved you," he said. "I wish I had . . ."

At that moment, as if responding to Chris's words, Soldier's hide rippled and he gave a little sigh. Then suddenly, the rasping breaths ceased.

Emily's face went white. She gaped at Neil, her hand to her mouth.

Neil shouted for the vet.

Mike pushed through into the intensive care unit moments later.

He moved up to the table and began feeling the dog with his hands. He lifted Soldier's head up very gently and looked into the dog's eyes. With a sigh he laid Soldier's head back down and pulled out the IV.

"He's gone, I'm afraid. There's nothing I can do

now. I'm sorry." He looked at Neil, standing next to him. "Find me when you're ready. I'll be outside."

Neil felt awful. He had never seen a dog die before. He'd had a pet dog before Sam, named Goldie, and he'd had to be put down. But Neil was so young then and hadn't been around when it had happened.

Neil felt furious and angry. It was so frustrating, not knowing who this dog had belonged to or why he had been so badly treated. *Somebody* was responsible for Soldier's death and, even though he couldn't do anything to bring him back, Neil was determined to find out who was to blame.

Mike Turner had a small pet cemetery in the hospital garden.

"If you'd like, we could bury Soldier there," he said. "We haven't found the owner and the poor dog will need a proper send-off."

Neil and his father discussed it with the rest of the family and they all agreed that it was the right thing to do.

Bob and Mike dug a grave beside a pear tree in one corner of the small garden.

Sarah had done a drawing of Soldier with wings and a lopsided halo — "So that he can go straight up to heaven," she announced. She gave it to her father so that it could be put into the grave with Soldier.

The dog's body, wrapped in a white cloth, was lowered gently into the hole in the ground.

Neil had intended to make a speech, but in the end he felt he couldn't. Chris volunteered himself.

"We are here today to honor the Unknown Soldier," he said, standing over the shallow grave. "Though wounded in battle, he fought bravely to the last. Good-bye, Soldier."

"Good-bye, Soldier," they all muttered.

There was silence while Mike solemnly filled in the hole and smoothed the surface over.

A crisp, brown leaf drifted from the big sycamore tree and landed on the grave. Sarah sobbed loudly and her mother put an arm around her.

"Thanks for everything, Mike," Carole said. "Wherever Soldier is now, I'm sure he's in a much happier place. Come on, you guys, let's go home."

"Well, I think we can safely say that Mr. Harding's not going to come for Jessie tonight," Bob Parker announced late that evening. "I've just tried the phone number he gave us. I got the 'nonworking number' message, so I checked with the operator. It's 'out of order,' according to her."

Neil bit his lip. Should he tell his dad what he and Kate had found out about Harding's address?

For the moment he decided to keep quiet. He wanted to work it out himself, and with everything else that had happened, the matter of 149 Dale End Road had slipped his mind. Anyway, they had all felt so positive that Harding *would* be back to pick up Jessie.

"What do we do now?" Neil inquired.

"Wait to see if he turns up tomorrow. His flight's probably been delayed."

Neil hoped his father was right — that it wasn't anything more serious than that.

Neil spent the following morning working on a school project. There was still no sign of Harding. At lunchtime, he decided to pay Jessie another visit, in case Harding came for her that afternoon and he didn't see her again. When he reached her pen, he got a terrible shock. There was a Yorkshire terrier in it instead of Jessie.

Neil ran to the kennel office. His mother was there, typing at the keyboard of the office computer.

"Where's Jessie, Mom?" he demanded.

"We've put her into the rescue center," she replied, looking at him over the top of the screen, an edge of weariness in her voice.

"No! You can't! She's not homeless!"

"We had no alternative, Neil. The kennels are fully booked, so we couldn't keep her where she was."

Neil didn't protest. He couldn't. He knew that what his mother said was right: If someone had booked a place for their dog, then Jessie had to move out to make room for it.

"Don't worry, Neil. You know she'll get the same care and attention. Think of it as just a change of hotel room."

Neil smiled, already feeling a bit better. "Yeah, OK, Mom. I'll go over and see her. Take her for a walk, maybe."

"Don't tire her out, OK? Let her dictate the pace. She'll tell you when she's had enough and wants to go home," his mother told him.

"Sure. See you later."

Jessie appeared to be settling into her new

quarters very well. When Neil arrived she was scratching and circling, building herself a really comfortable bed.

"Jessie, time for your walk," Neil called.

The dog looked up from her exertions and gave a little bark.

Neil unclipped her leash and opened the pen. Jessie sniffed at her handiwork, then walked obediently over to Neil.

It seemed a bit unfair not to take Sam, too. Neil knew he had been neglecting him slightly since Jessie's arrival. He called Sam's name and the Border collie came darting up to him.

The three of them were just crossing the courtyard when Chris stormed around the corner and through the side gate on his bike. He braked so violently that he skidded on the gravel stones before coming to a stop.

"Neil, quick! You've got to see this!" he shouted.

"See what?"

"Something totally weird that I just found. Something you're not going to believe!"

CHAPTER EIGHT

"**I**s it far?" Neil asked Chris. "I don't want to walk Jessie too far in her condition."

"In the woods," Chris said. "On the other side of the hill. I rode the long way back, down the road, but this way through the fields should be quicker."

Chris was leading the way on foot, with Neil following and keeping a close eye on Jessie. She seemed fine, keeping pace with Sam and even dashing off with him on one of his forays into a nearby hedge.

Neil could not get any information out of Chris about what he was taking him to see. All of his questions about whether it was connected with Soldier were met with stony silence and a "wait and see."

Chris took him to a thick patch of hilly woodland bordering an isolated house. They had never explored around there because the owners of the house had a dog with an exceedingly angry bark. It always seemed best to steer clear.

"It's just up here," said Chris.

"It's very steep," said Neil. "I think I'll leave Jessie here rather than drag her up this hill. Those mossy stones look really slippery. I wouldn't want her to fall."

He put on Jessie's leash and fastened it securely to a branch. She whined wistfully as the others plunged upward through the trees without her.

It was hard going. "What were you doing up here in the first place?" Neil asked.

"I was on the top road. There are some great paths up here for biking. Then I found —"

"Wow!" Neil interrupted, having suddenly glimpsed what Chris was about to show him. "How on earth did *that* get there?"

That was a white van. It was newish, too — not some old wreck that had been rotting in the woods for ages. Neil could see the dents and scratches it had suffered in its wild tumble down the slope. Gouged tree trunks and snapped branches marked its fall quite clearly.

The van was resting at an awkward angle, almost on its roof, pinned in place between some birch trees. "It can't have been here long. Look at the branches. Those breaks are fairly fresh," said Chris. "And it must have been pushed off the road that leads to the house."

"You don't think there's anyone in it, do you?" Neil was hesitant. He had awful visions of finding a dead body or someone with terrible injuries.

"I hope not," Chris replied grimly.

They pushed through the undergrowth and hauled their way up the steep slope, grabbing onto branches for extra support as the soles of their sneakers slipped on the damp rocks. Sam streaked effortlessly over the obstacles and reached the van ahead of them. He stood waiting for them, wagging his tail proudly.

"It's not locked," Chris pointed out. One of the doors had opened in the fall.

Neil paused, pressing his fingers over his lips as he thought hard. "Do you know something?" he said. "This van looks familiar."

"Yeah? From where? Do you think it's the one we saw on High Street?"

"Oh. Possibly. I was thinking more about Harding. He dropped Jessie off in a van like this. I remember noticing it."

"Well, if this *is* his van, where's Harding? He's late picking up Jess, isn't he?" said Chris.

"If he wasn't the businessman he said he was, but a detective investigating some crime — maybe the antiques robberies — then something may have happened to him. I think we'd better take a good look at that van."

"What about fingerprints, though? We don't want to destroy any evidence."

"We won't touch anything. Just look."

Wrapping the bottom of his sweatshirt around his hands, Chris heaved on the door and managed to get it open far enough for them to stick their heads inside. But before they got a chance, Sam had wriggled through into the cab.

He was out again almost instantly, growling, with something in his mouth.

"Ugh!" exclaimed Neil. "What have you got there? It looks like a dead animal!"

Chris had gone rather pale. "It looks more like a scalp," he said.

"Drop, Sam, drop!" Neil ordered and Sam obediently dropped the black, hairy object at his feet.

Neil touched it with his toe, then flipped it over.

"It *is* a scalp!" Chris said, recoiling in horror.

"No, it's not! It's some sort of wig. Look —"

He picked it up with his fingertips and held it out to Chris. Up close, they could see the artificial webbing to which the shiny black hair was attached. With a chill, almost uncanny sense of certainty, something fell into place.

"Perfectly shiny black hair . . ." he said. "*Too* perfect. Remember what I told you Sarah had said about Harding? The day he arrived? She said he had 'funny hair.' I noticed it, too. I bet our Mr. Harding was wearing a wig, and this is it!"

"A wig? But why would he be wearing a wig?"

"As part of his disguise. If he was a detective —"

"Hey, what if it was Harding driving that van the other night?" Chris broke in. "The driver had red hair, but it could still have been him. Maybe this is the van that nearly hit us!"

"Which means he was back in time to pick up Jessie —"

"Or that he never went away at all," Chris said. "Either way, I bet it's got something to do with that house. We're so close to finding the answer — I can feel it."

"Come on, we've got to look. But we can't leave Jessie. I'll go back and get her," Neil said.

Leaving Chris holding Sam's collar, he scrambled

back down the slope. Jessie was pleased to see him. She wagged her tail and gave a short, welcoming bark.

"Come on, girl," Neil told her. "We're going to take this very easy. I don't want you straining yourself."

He took the leash and tried to find the easiest route back to the van. He rejoined Chris and they let the dogs find their own way up, scrambling after them up the rough terrain.

"Sam? Jessie?" Neil called. He was rewarded with some urgent barks that drew them to a spot higher up, past the van, to a wall on which both dogs were standing, a wall with a large hole in it marked with white paint. A trail of churned-up earth and smashed plants led from it.

"At least we know where it came from," said Chris.

Jessie barked suddenly and sniffed the ground on the far side of the wall. She made a dash toward the house.

Close up, the house looked ramshackle. The roof had missing slates and a plant had rooted itself in the rain gutter. Yet the windows were all intact, not a broken pane among them. Chris noticed a burglar alarm set high up on one wall.

Jessie began scratching at the back door, whining and whimpering excitedly.

Chris looked at Neil. "What on earth could be in there that she's so interested in?" he said.

"Rats, probably. Now, how are we going to get into this place?"

"Do you really think we should break in?" asked Chris.

"Only if we have to. C'mon, let's look around."

Ordering Jessie to sit and be quiet, Neil tried the back door handle. The door was locked. They crept cautiously around to the front but there was still no sign of life.

The coast was clear. There was nothing in the front of the house other than a gravel driveway, a badly neglected garden, and a gate that opened onto a muddy, rutted road with high banks on either side. The front door was as securely locked as the back one.

Then they noticed a sign by the front gate. While Chris tried the door again, Neil went to investigate.

"Hey! It says BEWARE GUARD DOG," he told Chris. "There can't be one here, though, or it would have been barking by now."

"What are we going to do?" said Chris. "If we smash a window, we'll set off the alarm. Then we don't know *who* might come running up here to see what's going on."

"Looking at the state of that road, I hardly think anyone will be able to *run*," Neil replied. "And if the alarm is wired up to the police station, they're just the guys we want to see! Come on, don't be afraid. Find a way to get in."

"Those side windows looked old. Maybe one'll be unlocked, or we can force one open." Chris tried a couple of windows without success. "Let's try the front again."

Neil pushed at one of the large sash windows and was relieved when it moved a little. "Success!" he cried. "Give me a hand and we'll be able to make this opening bigger."

Pushing the window together, they soon made the opening big enough for them to climb through.

But before they could move, a streak of brown dog shot past them and leaped through the window. The moment she got inside, Jessie started barking — a wild, excited barking that they had never heard from her before. There was the sound of her paws thudding on wooden stairs. Suddenly the barking stopped.

Neil looked at Chris. "Come on," he said. "We're going in."

Gingerly, they squeezed through the window. Sam put his paws on the windowsill and heaved himself up and through.

They found themselves in a kitchen. The only furniture was a scratched old table and two rickety wooden chairs. A tap dripped monotonously into the cracked and stained enamel sink.

"It's a little scary, isn't it?" whispered Chris.

Sam followed his nose and padded up the stairs, sniffing at the ground as he went.

Neil nodded. "Scary isn't the word. Where's Sam going? Looks like he's found his tracking instinct at last."

"Come on, let's follow him. Get it over with. Jessie has to be up there."

Holding his finger to his lips, Neil motioned for Chris to follow him and they both gingerly crept up the stairs.

There were two doors off the landing, one closed, one half-open. Knowing that the dogs must have gone through the open door, they moved toward it. There were muffled noises and some dog sounds coming from inside, but nothing recognizable. Chris crept forward first and craned his head around the door to look inside.

Then he stepped back so rapidly that he nearly knocked Neil back down the stairs. "There's a man in there, lying on the floor," he whispered. "The dogs are beside him."

Neither of them said anything as they entered the room.

The man was lying on his side on a filthy, threadbare carpet. He was gagged, with his hands tied behind his back. Sam sat quietly next to him, but Jessie was licking his face ecstatically, her tail waving so fast that it was a blur in the dusty air. The man had red hair, but his distinctive, craggy face was familiar.

"Harding!" said Neil.

CHAPTER NINE

There was a desperate appeal in the eyes of the bound man as he looked straight at Neil and Chris.

"Better get that gag off him. He looks like he's going to suffocate," said Chris.

The gag was a grubby black scarf and the knot was tight. Harding moaned and moved his head as Neil worked at untying it.

"I wonder how long he's been here?" Chris looked on anxiously as Neil forced his fingernails into the knot. Harding certainly didn't look like a smart businessman now. His lips were dry and deathly white where the tight material had compressed them, and his face was rough with dark stubble.

Neil gave up wrestling with the knot and Chris

rushed down to the kitchen to see if he could find a knife. He came back with a bread knife.

Neil sawed at the knot until the last thread parted.

Harding ran a dry tongue over the cracked skin around his mouth. "Water," he whispered. "Give me water."

This time it was Neil who went down to the kitchen. He filled a chipped mug at the sink but as he did so, he kicked something heavy at his feet. Looking down, he noticed a piece of bubble wrap sticking out of a half-open cupboard door.

Opening the cupboard, Neil saw four lidless cardboard boxes, each containing articles wrapped in the same protective packaging. He pulled the nearest box out and saw something silver gleaming through the clear bubble wrap. A thrill shot through him as he reached for the object and gently parted the wrap. He knew nothing about antiques, but the ornate pattern on the silver coffeepot he held in his hands, and the weight of it, convinced him that he held something very valuable.

As he was beginning to think what his discovery meant, a sound came from the room above him, a heavy, dragging, thumping sound. Neil felt cold pricks of alarm raise all the hairs on the back of his neck. He gripped the mug and ran up the stairs three at a time.

As Neil entered the room, Chris was about to cut the rope that bound Harding's wrists.

"No!" Neil yelled. "Don't untie him!"

Chris looked at Neil as if he were mad. "But he's been tied up for days! He must be in pain."

Harding nodded, his eyes glued to the mug of water. He licked his dry lips. "Please," he said, again in a low, raspy voice.

"It wouldn't do any harm . . ." Chris appealed to Neil.

"We don't know what's happened here yet. We may need to get the police."

"How's he going to drink the water?"

"Like this," Neil said. He put the mug on the floor. "Give me a hand."

Together, they tugged the heavy man back into a sitting position with his back against the wall. Jessie promptly leaned against him. It was as if she couldn't possibly get close enough to her owner. Neil raised the water to Harding's lips. He drained the mug in huge, greedy gulps.

"More, please," he croaked, his voice parched from thirst. "I haven't had a thing, food or water, for three days. You haven't got any food, have you?"

"Only these," said Chris, pulling half a packet of mints out of his pocket.

"Untie my hands, boys. Please. I've got no feeling in my fingers," Harding whispered. "Or my feet."

Neil looked down and saw that Harding's ankles were bound with rope, too — very tightly.

Jessie whined and nudged her owner. "Just let me stroke my dog," Harding begged in another cracked whisper. "I haven't seen her for a week. She's looking good. You've obviously looked after her well."

Neil felt torn. If it were him lying there, he'd want to give Jessie a proper greeting. What harm would it do to untie him? In such a weak condition, he could hardly run away!

Chris put some mints in Harding's mouth and, as the man began to chew them noisily, Neil picked up the mug and went downstairs to refill it. Chris came after him.

"Look, let's untie him just for a while, so he can get more comfortable," Chris said. "It seems cruel not to. Half a packet of mints in three days is hardly going to fuel him enough for a two-mile run to Compton. He'd probably collapse! Anyway, he hasn't told us why he's here yet. What if he is working for the police, Neil?"

"Surely he would have told us right away, if he was," Neil pointed out. "He'd have told us where to find his ID. And what about all this stuff?" Neil flicked open the cupboard under the sink to reveal the stash of silver and antique valuables. "How's he going to explain that?"

Chris rummaged through the boxes and was at a

loss for words. "He's probably still out of it from being tied up," he said after a few moments, ". . . wondering if he was going to starve to death, or die of thirst."

Neil wasn't convinced.

"Let's ask him a few questions, and then make up our minds," Chris suggested.

"OK," Neil agreed.

They took him the water. Again, he swiftly drained it.

"Thanks," he said, his voice a little clearer and stronger.

Neil sat down on the floor, about two feet away from Harding. He crossed his legs and folded his arms. Sam sat obediently by his side. "Okay. You obviously haven't been in Tokyo, so what exactly have you been doing?" he demanded.

Harding shook his head. "This and that. Business things," he said.

"What sort of business things get you tied up and dumped in an empty house?" he demanded.

"Not quite empty," Chris reminded him. "There are a few interesting items downstairs."

Harding groaned as he wriggled and tried to ease his cramped arms. "Now, come on, boys, stop playing games," he said. "Untie me and let me take Jessie home. Then we can talk to the police. What were you intending to do? Go off and leave me here? What if those thugs who tied me up come back for me?"

Neil looked at Chris. Which thugs? Neither of them knew what to do. Then Neil took charge again.

"Those items in the kitchen look like antiques to me," he said. "Could all this have something to do with the robberies that have been taking place recently?"

Neil watched Harding's face closely as he spoke. He gave a slight smile, raised his eyebrows, and replied smoothly, "That's very clever of you, kid. You'll grow up to make a good detective."

"Like you?" Chris said.

"Shh!" Neil hissed fiercely. If Harding wasn't a detective after all, then Chris had just put the idea into his head.

"I was right. You're both clever. You've put two and two together and come to exactly the right conclusion. I am a detective. The story about my business trip was a lie and I was actually investigating the robberies. I was posing as a crooked antiques dealer interested in buying some of the stolen goods cheap," said Harding. His explanation sounded as if it might be true.

"Why did you wear a wig when you brought Jessie to us?" asked Neil.

"There aren't many redheaded detectives around. They would have found out who I was. I'm quite well known."

"Wouldn't it have been easier to dye your real hair?" Chris inquired.

"Maybe, but not so easy to *keep* it dyed when you're on a case for weeks on end. The wig seemed simpler. But they spotted me without the damn thing on one day, and realized I wasn't all that I seemed."

"What happened?" Chris was beginning to come around to this version of events. He listened intently.

"They were on to me then," Harding continued, "and it was only a matter of time before they discovered through their contacts that I was a detective from the London Police. We had a fight and I ended up here, trussed up like a turkey."

"Why didn't they just kill you, rather than leave you tied up?" Neil asked.

"Killing a policeman is a very serious offense. If they left me here, there was a chance I might be found," Harding explained. "Look, I'm starving, boys. Do I really have to answer all these questions?"

"Only a few more," Neil promised, playing for time while he continued to think about what to do. "Is that your van that we found pushed down the hill?"

"Yes," replied Harding. "After they caught me, they hid it."

"So was that you zigzagging through Compton the other night with a black BMW in tow?"

"Yes. They had guns. They were after me. I managed to lose them, but they caught up with me later."

"You nearly ran into us!" said Neil, his voice quivering a little. "Didn't you see us?"

"I did at the last moment. I didn't know it was you. Sorry . . ." Harding gave them an apologetic look, then groaned again, shaking his legs. "Come on, get these ankles of mine free. It's vital that I contact the police as soon as possible. I'm the only one who knows where the stolen goods are now. I haven't got my cellular phone, I lost it in the struggle — as I was trying to get away from them. You do believe me, don't you?"

"Go on, Neil," said Chris.

Neil frowned. Harding's story *was* very convincing. A whimper from Jessie made him look down to where she was lying, snuggled up against her owner. She shifted onto her side and began licking herself. In that position, he could see her swollen belly clearly.

Sam was still sitting nearby on the floor, watching Jessie and Neil.

Harding followed Neil's eyes and saw him looking at Sam. "I remember him from that night I brought Jessie around to you. He looks like a fantastic dog. By the way, you didn't see a dog outside anywhere, did you? There was a guard dog here."

Chris shook his head. "There was no dog here when we arrived," he said.

"He got hurt in the struggle when the gang captured me. I've been really worried about him."

"What did he look like, this guard dog? Neil's parents run a dog rescue center, you know, and there's a chance he might have been brought in."

"He was a Doberman cross. Brown and black. I only saw him once, when they dragged me here. They called him Brandy."

Harding's words thudded into Neil's brain as he stared at Chris. A wounded black-and-brown Doberman cross. The description fit poor Soldier exactly.

"A dog like that *was* brought into the center," Neil said slowly.

"He's alive! Great! I've been worried about him. I don't like people harming dogs." Harding smiled for the first time.

"You seem to care an awful lot about a dog you don't even know," said Neil.

Harding said nothing.

Jessie whimpered again.

"The dog's dead," Chris said savagely. "He was shot. He lost a lot of blood. Then he got pneumonia and died."

Harding flinched as if he had been kicked. He blinked several times and his pale face grew even paler. "I tried to stop them," he said. "I tried to make Brandy go for them. When I saw Jamieson point the gun, I tried to deflect the shot. It went wide, but I knew his leg had been hit. All this time I've been hoping he might have gotten to safety and that he wasn't injured too badly . . ."

Harding's voice choked. Neil stared at him. Instinct was telling him that there was more to it than this. "Why did you try so hard to protect the dog when you were fighting for your own life?" He spoke slowly, trying to get his racing thoughts in some sort of order. "And if he was a guard dog and you were a stranger, why didn't he turn on you? Why should he have obeyed you and attacked them?"

Harding bit his lip and looked away, then met Neil's gaze again.

"OK, OK. I'll tell you. Brandy was my dog. I trained him. I trained both him and Jessie from the time they were puppies. I used to be a police dog handler. Jessie's an Airedale cross, the first I ever trained. We found that crossbreeds often trained more easily than pedigrees. Brandy's — I mean, Brandy was . . ."

Harding looked crumpled, but continued. "He was a fantastic animal," he said softly. "He'd do anything for me, obey any order. I was a fool to let them near him. I —"

"Jessie!" The shout from Chris caught everybody's attention.

Neil looked down at Jessie, and crouched down by her side. Jessie's head was down and poked forward. She was panting and her sides were heaving.

"Chris," Neil gasped. "I think her puppies are coming!"

CHAPTER TEN

Harding spoke again, his voice hard and full of authority.

"OK, you two, stop messing around and release me. Come on. This is serious now. Jessie's my dog and her puppies look like they're being born early. If anything happens to them, you'll pay for this!"

"Chris, you get the police and I'll stay here."

"No!" The word exploded into the quiet air of the empty house like a pistol shot. "Just untie me, that's all you need to do. We'll get help for Jessie and then we'll go to the police."

Neil glared at Harding and continued giving hurried instructions to Chris. "Tell them that as well as having somebody here that they're looking for, we've also got a dog about to give birth. They've got to call Dad at the kennels, or Mike Turner."

"I don't understand . . ." Chris stared at Harding with a puzzled expression, then glanced back at Neil. "I thought he was a detective . . ."

"You fell for that story?" Neil asked and shook his head. "Didn't you listen, Chris? Our Mr. Harding here gave himself away."

"How?" Chris asked. Harding was keeping quiet, gazing anxiously at the panting Jessie.

"Harding used to be a dog trainer all right, but he was never a detective. Soldier — I mean Brandy — was being used as a guard dog by the thieves. And why doesn't he want us to call the police, eh? I think he wore that wig when he brought Jessie in precisely so that the police — or anyone else — wouldn't see him and recognize him. Harding's in this up to his neck."

"But I still don't see —"

"Chris, *go!*"

Chris ran out of the room and tore down the stairs. Neil heard his footsteps race across the stones outside and clatter down the road. There was a farmhouse about a quarter of a mile away and Neil guessed he would go straight there to call the police.

As soon as Chris had left, Harding seemed to change. His main concern was about Jessie now, rather than his own fate.

"I don't know what's going to happen to me," he told Neil. "Someone's going to have to take care of her. And the puppies."

Gone was the smooth wiliness of earlier on. It had been replaced by the type of person Neil could understand: a dog lover.

"OK," he agreed. "So long as you do something for me."

"What's that?" Harding asked, sounding surprised.

"Just tell me the truth. You're not a detective, are you?"

"No."

"You're one of the gang of antiques thieves."

"Yes."

"So what really happened to make them tie you up and dump you?"

Harding heaved a deep sigh. "Greed," he admitted. "I wanted a bigger share of the money for myself, so I tried to double-cross them. I was planning to hijack one of the truckloads of stolen goods and make it seem like a police raid. I could have sold it and made a fortune."

Neil whistled. "So you were going to rob the robbers!"

"Yep. I thought I'd won their trust, but I hadn't. They'd been monitoring the calls I made on my cellular phone while I was finding buyers for the stuff myself. They hid me here while they decided what to do."

"Why did they have to kill Brandy?" Neil wanted to know.

"I told you that dog would have done anything for me. They were worried that I might have got some signal to him to go and get help, or something. Or that I might order him to attack them. I could have done both. So it was safest for them to gag me and kill him."

"We gave him a proper funeral, you know," said Neil. "We didn't know his name. We called him Soldier. He's buried in the vet's garden."

"Thanks for telling me that."

Harding gave Neil such a grave, penetrating look that Neil knew he was talking from the heart. There was silence for a few moments as Neil remembered Soldier, and Harding remembered Brandy.

"They were going to come back for that Georgian silver tonight, you know. It's a good thing you found me, really. Who knows what they might have done to me."

"So we saved your life?"

Harding nodded. "I suppose a few years in prison is better than being dead."

Jessie's panting stopped for a moment. She looked up at her master and Neil saw the worry in Harding's eyes.

"She'll be all right. Chris will be back soon," he said. "Then we'll get her right over to the kennels."

"If I get put in jail, Neil, I'll never see the puppies. It's Jessie's first litter, too. I would have given anything to see those puppies."

Neil bit his lip. It seemed an impossible situation.

They heard the sound of sirens in the distance. "It's the police," said Neil.

"Oh Jess," Harding said, gazing down at the dog lying on the floor. "I'm going to miss you, girl. I'm really going to miss you."

Emily came running out when she saw the police car approaching.

"Go and find Mom or Dad, quick, it's an emergency!" Neil yelled. He climbed out of the backseat, where he had been sitting with Chris and Jessie. He opened the passenger door and Sam bounded out and into the house.

Emily dashed off and soon Bob Parker appeared, a worried look on his face.

"What's wrong? There hasn't been an accident, has there?" he asked the police officer.

"It's Jessie, Dad. Her puppies are coming. They're early."

Bob Parker and Neil lifted Jessie gently from the car. Her sides were rigid and they could feel the spasms as she got ready to push the puppies out.

"We might have to get Mike Turner over here —

there may be complications. Emily, run and tell your mom about Jessie," Bob said. Then, seeing Neil and Chris climb back into the police car, he exclaimed, "Hey, you two, where are you going?"

"We've got to give statements," Chris told him. "We found Mr. Harding. He was one of the antiques robbers."

"You'd better follow us down to the station, sir," one of the officers told an astounded Mr. Parker. "And we'd better get hold of the other boy's parents, too."

Giving the statements took a long time. Neil had to begin his version of events from the moment Mr.

Harding brought Jessie to the kennels. The police
wanted to know the exact time to the minute, so they
could try to work out his movements that evening.
They also wanted to know all about Soldier.

"We've had our eye on Harding for some time," the
Detective Sergeant told them. "He's from Compton
originally. His sister still lives here, on Dale End
Road."

Chris and Neil looked at each other.

"He went to London and became a dog handler for
the police, but got kicked out for receiving stolen
goods — stereos from a big warehouse raid. He got a
suspended sentence. He disappeared for a while after that and we thought he must have gone legit. But
we were wrong. Now, tell me exactly where that van
is. Oh, and we'll need to get that wig, for evidence."

All the time they were in the police station, Neil's
thoughts were with Jessie. He remembered Harding's words about it being his fault if anything happened to her and the puppies. Perhaps it *was* his
fault for having taken her on that walk; for having
got her into a situation where she had overdone
things; shocking her body into delivering her puppies too soon. He couldn't wait to get home and see
how she was.

When he finally arrived, his mother said that the
puppies still hadn't been born.

Sarah and Emily were allowed to visit Jessie's pen

before they went off to bed, but their father wouldn't let them go in. "You mustn't crowd her," he explained. "She needs plenty of space."

He examined Jessie gently while Neil watched with growing anxiety. "I don't like the way she's looking so distressed," he said. "I'm going to give Mike Turner a call and get him to come and check her over."

Neil sat by Jessie's side, stroking her and talking to her, hardly aware how late it was getting. Soon Emily crept back to join him, wearing an anorak over her nightgown.

"Mom said I could come. I couldn't sleep worrying about her," Emily whispered.

It was almost ten-thirty when Mike Turner strode into the center with Mr. and Mrs. Parker. Neil and Emily moved out of Jessie's pen so that he could examine her.

"I don't think these puppies are early," he said. "They seem full size to me. The first pup is the biggest one and it feels as if it's got stuck. That's why nothing's happening. As this is her first litter, I'd feel happier doing a Caesarean."

"What's that?" Emily asked.

"It's an operation to take the puppies out," said Mike. "It's sometimes necessary when the mother isn't able to give birth by herself."

Everyone exchanged anxious glances.

"Don't worry," Mike said. "It's a common operation, and Jessie will soon recover. I'll have to take her back to the hospital with me, though."

"Do you have to?" Neil pleaded.

"It really would be safer for Jessie and easier for me," Mike replied. "We've got special equipment and drugs back at the operating room. I hope I won't need them, but they're there in case I do."

Neil watched Jessie being carried out to Mike's Range Rover. Even though she was a large dog, on the special stretcher Mike used she looked frail and very weak.

"I'll let you know as soon as there's any news," called Mike, waving to them from the open window of his vehicle as he pulled away.

"OK, let's close up shop," said Mr. Parker as they watched the tail lights of the vehicle disappear. "Jessie's in good hands, now. Worrying about her is not going to help her one bit."

The following day, vacation was over and Neil had to go back to school. He didn't know how he got through his lessons that day. Twice his teachers had to tell him to pay attention and, to make matters worse, Mr. Hamley gave him an extra essay to write for homework, on the subject of daydreaming.

When he finally got home after that endless day, he found the rest of his family sitting around the kitchen table. His mother and father had mugs of coffee and Sarah and Emily were drinking orange soda. None of them looked the slightest bit anxious or depressed.

Neil frowned. "Hey, what's with you guys?" he asked accusingly. "How could you look happy when poor Jessie's going through a horrible operation!"

He felt like a real outsider as they all looked at one another and grinned.

"We know something you don't!" Sarah piped up.

"Come on, let's put him out of his misery," his mother said. "She's had three puppies, Neil. Two females and a male. Mother and babies are all doing well, as they say. We're celebrating!"

"When can I see them?" Neil asked excitedly.

"Jessie's going to stay at the vet's tonight, just to make sure that there are no last-minute complications, but we can pick her up tomorrow."

"Yes!" Neil punched the air with excitement. "I have to tell Chris," he yelled, racing toward the telephone.

When Neil got home from school the following afternoon, he went straight to the rescue center. His mother told him where to find Jessie. They had made up a special maternity pen for her.

His father was already there, having just given Jessie some food.

Quietly, his heart thudding in excitement, Neil moved into Jessie's pen. The dog lay contentedly on her side, sleepy and warm under the special heat lamp that Bob Parker had hung inside the pen. Nuzzling close to their mother, blind and velvety-skinned, were three fat little puppies.

"They look like moles!" he laughed.

"They'll soon grow their coats, don't you worry," Bob Parker reassured him.

Neil stroked Jessie's head gently.

"Will she be able to feed the puppies OK with that scar?" he asked eventually. He could clearly see the shaved area on her abdomen and the line of stitches from her operation.

"Oh, yes," said his father. "And she'll have the stitches taken out in ten days. By that time the puppies will probably have their eyes open."

They watched the puppies squirm against Jessie's side, pummeling her with their tiny paws and making little squeaking noises. Jessie turned her head to lick them while they sucked noisily at her teats. One puppy — the largest — kept pushing the others aside.

"That one's going to be a little bruiser," commented Mr. Parker.

"I suppose that's the leader," said Neil. He stared at it. Did it have a slight look of Doberman?

"That's the one that caused all the trouble. He was too big to come out."

Neil could have stayed there watching for hours, but he had homework to do, so he locked up his bike and went inside to join Sarah and Emily, who were having their snack.

"I hope Jessie and her babies can stay with us for always!" said Sarah.

"I know, honey," said Carole, "but it's just not possible. Her owner's sister has telephoned. She's coming to collect Jessie and the puppies as soon as they can be moved."

"She lives on Dale End Road, doesn't she?" Neil asked.

"Yes. Why?" asked his mother.

"You don't by any chance remember which number, do you?"

"I'm pretty sure it was one-forty-seven. I'll go and check . . ."

She went off to the office and came back with the card. "See? One-forty-seven. I was right!"

Neil seized the card. "That looks like a nine, not a seven," he observed.

"Yes, it does a bit, doesn't it? But I know it's a seven. It's my horrible, wiggly writing. Normally, I'd have typed it, but it was so late and I couldn't be bothered turning on the electric typewriter."

Neil sighed, thinking what Kate and Chris were going to say about the clue that never was!

"Harding's sister has asked us to help her find homes for the puppies," his mother said.

"He's never going to see them, is he?" Neil said. "He'll be in prison."

"That's where he ought to be, too. He's a crook!" Emily pointed out.

"But he loved Jessie. And Brandy. And they loved him. I don't think anyone who loves dogs can be all that bad," Neil said. "Do you?"

He gazed at the faces of his family, looking from one to the other, daring them to disagree. But nobody did. They all remained silent, even Sarah.

Suddenly, Neil found that he couldn't eat anymore, and tossed his half-eaten toast into the garbage. He felt choked up. What if Harding spent so long in prison that Jessie grew old and died and he never saw her again?

Just then, Neil felt a familiar wet nose pushing its way into his hand. It was Sam, who had squeezed his way in to see what all the fuss was about and was demanding attention.

Neil shook his head, as if to clear it of all other dogs. He went to fetch his coat.

"Come on, Sam," he said. "You know none of them are as good as you. Tomorrow, we're going to start training you again and next summer you're going to win that Agility course paws down, or I'm not the best dog trainer in Compton!"